Richard Scarry's
A Day at the Police Station

A Random House PICTUREBACK® Book

RANDOM HOUSE 🏠 NEW YORK

Copyright © 2004 by the Richard Scarry Corporation. All rights reserved.
Published in the United States by Random House Children's Books,
a division of Random House, Inc., New York.

PICTUREBACK, RANDOM HOUSE and colophon, and PLEASE READ TO ME and colophon
are registered trademarks of Random House, Inc.

Library of Congress Cataloging-in-Publication Data
Scarry, Richard. A day at the police station / Richard Scarry. p. cm.
SUMMARY: Bridget spends a day at work with her father, Sergeant Murphy,
and learns what an important job being a police officer is.
ISBN 978-0-375-82822-5
[1. Police—Fiction.   2. Police stations—Fiction.   3. Fathers and daughters—Fiction.
4. Dogs—Fiction.   5. Animals—Fiction.]   I. Title.   PZ7.S324Dayg 2004   [E]—dc22   2003015739

www.randomhouse.com/kids

Printed in the United States of America   15 14 13 12 11 10 9 8 7 6

It is Friday evening.
The Murphy family has finished
dinner. Mrs. Murphy clears the table
while Sergeant Murphy washes
the dishes.

"It's time to get into your
pajamas and go off to bed,"
Mrs. Murphy tells Bridget.

"Run along up to your room and I'll read
you a story!" calls Sergeant Murphy.

While Bridget climbs the stairs, she can hear her parents talking in the kitchen.

"I have to go to Workville tomorrow, Sarge," says Mrs. Murphy. "Could you please look after Bridget?"

"Hmmm," replies Sergeant Murphy. "Officer Flo is sick. I have to be on duty for her tomorrow—but I'll just take Bridget to the police station with me. She won't mind, I think."

But when Sergeant Murphy goes up to Bridget's room, he finds her crying.

"What's the matter, Bridget?" Sergeant Murphy asks.

"I wanted to go to the amusement park tomorrow," Bridget cries. "And now you have to work! I don't like that you're a police officer. You're ALWAYS on duty!"

"But being a police officer is very important," says Sergeant Murphy, hugging Bridget. "I'm sorry we can't go to the amusement park, but we'll have a good time at the police station. THAT I can promise!"

The next morning,
Sergeant Murphy and Bridget
drive off to the police station.
"Goodbye, Bridget!" calls
Mrs. Murphy. "Goodbye, Sarge!"

On the way, they
come to an intersection.
There is a huge traffic jam!
The traffic light
is broken.

Sergeant Murphy
directs the cars
until Mr. Fixit
can come and
repair the light.

"This is what Daddy calls
a good time?" Bridget says, pouting.
"Watching traffic?"

Just then, Mr. Raccoon
comes out of his coffee shop,
bringing Bridget a glass
of milk and a donut.

"Your father sure does a great job, Bridget!" he says.
"I don't know what Busytown would do without him."

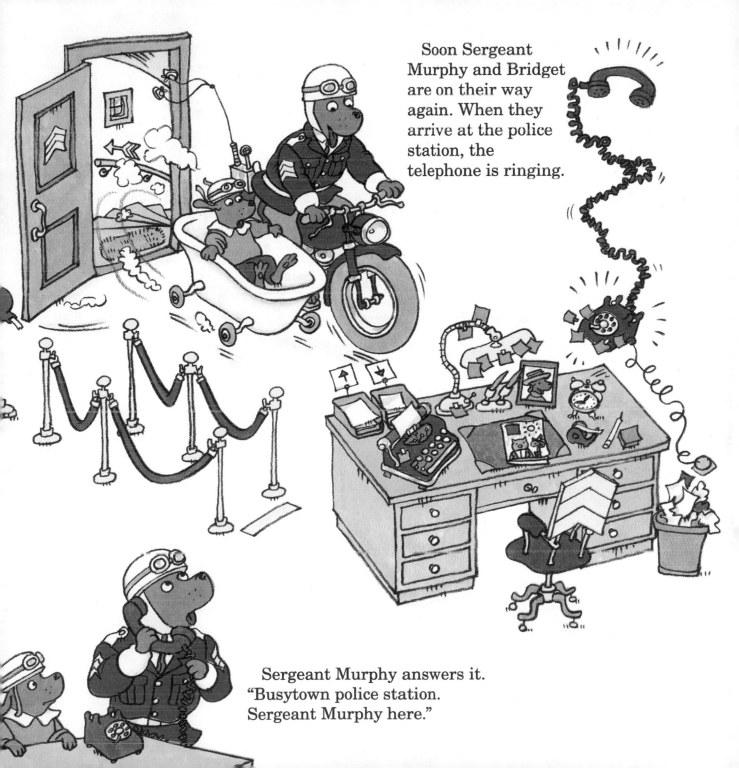

Soon Sergeant Murphy and Bridget are on their way again. When they arrive at the police station, the telephone is ringing.

Sergeant Murphy answers it. "Busytown police station. Sergeant Murphy here."

It's Hilda Hippo on the line.

"Oh, Sergeant Murphy, I'm so frightened!
There's a ghost in my bathroom!"
"A GHOST?" Sergeant Murphy replies.
"Just stay calm, Hilda. I'll be right over!"

Sergeant Murphy
and Bridget race over to Hilda's.

When they arrive, Hilda looks as pale as a ghost herself.

"Sergeant Murphy, I haven't slept a wink!" Hilda says nervously. "The ghost has been flushing the toilet all night!"

Suddenly, from upstairs comes:
FLUSH!

"Hmmm," says Sergeant Murphy. "You two wait here while I see about this—er—ghost."

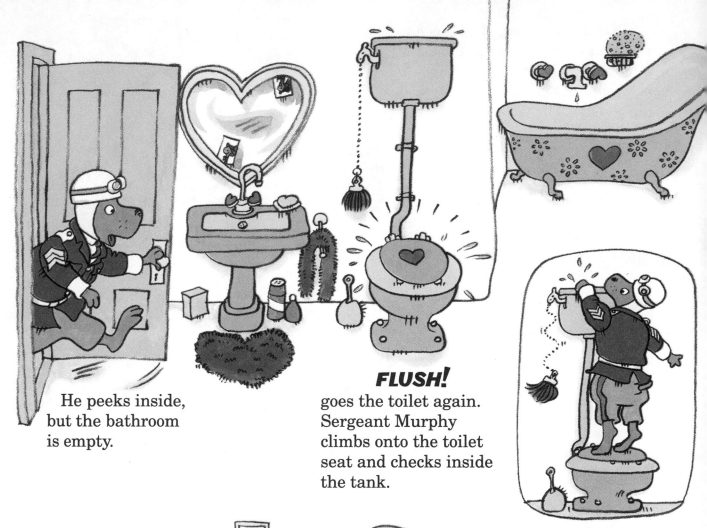

He peeks inside,
but the bathroom
is empty.

FLUSH!

goes the toilet again.
Sergeant Murphy
climbs onto the toilet
seat and checks inside
the tank.

"There!" he says.

"The toilet just needed some
adjusting. You shouldn't let your
imagination run away with you
like that, Hilda!"

On the way back to the police station, they
see a toddler crying in the street.

Sergeant Murphy takes her to the police station.

The phone is ringing when they
arrive. It's the child's mother!
Thank goodness her darling is safe
with Sergeant Murphy. Bridget
plays with the toddler until
her mother comes to fetch her.

Just then, Mr. Frumble arrives at the door. "Excuse me, but has anyone seen my hat?" he asks. "It's the third one I've lost in three days!"

Sergeant Murphy makes a note of the lost hat and promises to call Mr. Frumble if it's found.

Minutes after Mr. Frumble leaves, Mr. Gronkle storms in.

"I'm here to report a robbery!" he shouts.

"Wow! A real robbery!" thinks Bridget.

"My car keys have been stolen," says Mr. Gronkle, "and I know who took them: Wolfgang Wolf, Harry Hyena, and Benny Baboon!"

Through the door come Wolfgang, Harry, and Benny—each wearing a green hat.

"Did somebody call us?" asks Wolfgang.

"We found these hats," says Harry.

"And we're bringing them here to be returned to their rightful owner!" adds Benny.

"I saw you thieves walking around my car," shouts Mr. Gronkle. "You must have stolen my keys! I can't find them anywhere!"

"Now, just a moment, Mr. Gronkle!" Sergeant Murphy says. "You have to have some proof before you can accuse someone of stealing."

"We didn't take your keys!" says Wolfgang.
"We'd never steal anything!" says Harry.
"Honest!" adds Benny.

Sergeant Murphy decides they should all go together to the scene of the crime.

"Are THESE your stolen keys?"
Bridget asks Mr. Gronkle,
holding up a ring of keys.

"Why, yes!" replies
Mr. Gronkle, surprised.
"Wherever did you
find them?"

"Under your car, by the door," says Bridget.

"I guess your 'thief' must have accidentally
dropped them," Sergeant Murphy tells
Mr. Gronkle.
"I owe you an apology," Mr. Gronkle
says to Wolfgang, Harry, and Benny.
"To make up for my mistake, I want to
take you out for sundaes."

As they walk back to the police station, Sergeant Murphy and Bridget see two boys fighting.

Sergeant Murphy runs up and pulls them apart. "Stop that!" he says. "What's this all about?"

"Jimmy won't let me ride his bike!" says Johnny.
"It's MY bike!" shouts Jimmy.

"You need to settle your problems peacefully," Sergeant Murphy tells the boys.

Just then, Bridget hears someone crying, "HELP!"

Sergeant Murphy races
to the edge of the pier.
He bravely dives into
the river!

Sergeant Murphy carries
Bananas Gorilla safely out of
the river.
My, isn't he strong!

Then he dives back into the river!
Does he want to go for a swim?

No! He wants to get
Bananas's Bananamobile!
"Please do be careful
when driving near the water,"
Sergeant Murphy tells
Bananas.

Back at the police
station, Sergeant Murphy
puts on a dry uniform.
"We have to hurry, or we'll
be late for school!" he says.

Bridget is confused.
"School? On Saturday?" she wonders.

Sergeant Murphy and Bridget arrive at the school playground. Some children have come with their bikes for a traffic safety class.

Here are some of the things Sergeant Murphy teaches them:

Ride single file.

Always obey traffic lights and signals.

Give hand signals when turning.

Cross the street at the crosswalk.

Wear a helmet!

Make sure your brakes, lights, and bell work properly.

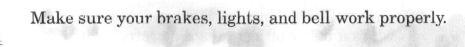

And please don't leave
your bike lying around.

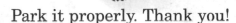

Park it properly. Thank you!

"We missed you at the amusement park today, Bridget," Huckle says.
"I was on duty with Daddy all day!" Bridget replies. "We got rid of a
ghost and helped a little girl find her mommy. Then we solved a robbery,
and Daddy stopped two boys who were fighting. Then he bravely saved
Bananas Gorilla from drowning!"

"Wow!" says Huckle. "Having a dad who's a police officer must be pretty neat!"

"You bet it is!" replies Bridget. "I think my daddy has the very best job EVER!"

"Um—excuse me, Sergeant Murphy, but has anyone seen my hat yet?"